Rejected
A Collection of Short Works
V. H. Mizzell

V. H. Mizzell Publishing

Contents

Foreword

You need to read this.

A lot of people don't read forwards, they skip them. That would be a mistake because if you skip this forward you may not notice in time what is going on. This is a short story collection. Not just any short story collection but an assortment of odds and ends that I have written in the last few years trying in dilettante fashion to get published in magazines.

These stories were all rejected by magazine publishers.

I am publishing them here because I can. And because I believe that your taste might be more informed and more important to me than some obscure magazine editor's taste.

If you like these stories please rate and comment and support my work by *buying something*. The paperback version perhaps.

Please do not troll me in the ratings and comments.

A Beautiful Day in a Perfect World

B ob had a virtual conference scheduled today. Many people regarded virtual conferences as an interruption to their work. Bob didn't, he looked forward to them. It was a welcome interruption to speak to another living being. Something Bob did not ordinarily do. It wasn't necessary to speak to anyone other than his robots on an ordinary day. They performed all the housework and maintenance, all the cooking and cleaning and grocery shopping. Everything he needed was delivered anyway.

His home office was well lit. Lots of sunlight and space. Simplicity and elegance. That's what he told the designers on the website he used to custom design his home. A long room with a big picture window, simple, elegant but still functional furniture.

He stood up to walk over to the window. Outside the golden sun glowed bright. It gave a panoramic view of the valley the little house sat in and the range of mountains beyond. Blue sky mottled with white cirrus, green grasses that stretched all the way to tree covered mountains. The outline of a creek cutting across the valley.

The weather was perfect. It was always perfect. Now that the world had weather control, each day was perfect. Bob was old enough to remember what it was like before weather control. The constant threat of storms, the unpredictability, the dread of the possibility of global climate change.

It made him want to go outside.

"I want to go outside Arthur."

The robot sat resting and recharging in an alcove designed for that purpose. At the sound of his master's voice he powered up and stood up. Arthur walked over to stand just behind Bob on his right side.

"You will have to put on your environment suit to go outside Bob", Arthur said, "the threat of viruses is high today."

"I don't care. Go and get it for me and help me into it. I've got to get outside today."

"You have a virtual conference today at thirteen hundred thirty hours."

"I don't care. I know you will remind me in time to come back in and attend it. Besides, you know how much I love speaking to collaborators. I sometimes go for days without speaking to anyone."

"As you wish Bob. I will remind you in time to make it back for the virtual conference. Fifteen minutes prior?"

"Yes. Yes, that's plenty. I am well prepared for this one."

Arthur turned to retrieve the environment suit.

• • • ● •● • ● • ● • • •

Bob and Arthur walked together across the green field. They didn't speak. Robots never speak unless spoken to. Some robots were programmed to be chatty but Bob didn't like that. The conversations didn't seem real somehow. All they could really do was respond and mirror. They had no original thoughts of their own. No observations to make.

Lost in his memories, Bob remembered how it was before weather control. How you could get caught in a summer shower. As a little boy he used to dam up rainwater in gutters and make mud pies, before everyone had to wear environment suits. He could remember the time before environment suits too, though it was long ago.

Now it only rained at night and early in the morning and only when necessary. A gentle misting rain, never heavy, never any lightning or wind. He slept through it most nights.

He missed it. Bob missed the rain. He wished he could feel it again.

"Bob, the farther we go in this direction the longer it will take us to get back in time. I suggest that we circle the house instead."

"No Arthur. I want to go and see the creek. I'd like to look at the creek and wade in the creek today. We have enough time don't we?"

"We do. But we can only loiter there for forty-five minutes before we should start back. Otherwise you will arrive late for your virtual conference."

"Fine. That's fine. Keep timing me."

The creek flowed gently along. Clear water mostly, tinted brown in the deeper spots. Things lived in it, swam in it, drank from it. A bird waded in it looking for minnows. Bob could see minnows furtively darting through its shallows. In the deeper parts some species of fish hovered about. A turtle popped it's head up to look at him downstream, then it ducked down to swim away.

A doe suddenly appeared out of the wood upstream like a specter and regarded them suspiciously. She just stared at the two of them for a bit before losing interest, then stepped forward to take a drink.

Bob felt peaceful and relaxed for the first time in a long while now. If only there were a way to safely remove the environment suit.

"We have to go back now Bob."

"What? We just got here! It hasn't been forty-five minutes!"

"Nevertheless we must go now to return in time."

"Gee whiz you never let me have any fun!"

Arthur did not understand the sarcasm in that remark. He was not programmed to understand wit, sarcasm, or irony. He did not respond verbally but turned to go then turned back to make sure Bob followed him.

They got back just in time. Bob entered the little cubicle and put his headset on. Everyone had gathered around a large meeting table or so it seemed. They were really all in their home offices, just as he was.

Bob didn't join in the conversation, he just let everyone talk without interrupting or asking questions. He felt a sense of togetherness even when he didn't interact directly with anyone.

When the virtual conference reached its conclusion a message popped up on Bob's screen. It was from his supervisor, Cynthia.

It said, "Bob, I would like to have a private meeting with you now, if you have some time. It's about a personnel matter."

The scene changed, they were now in Cynthia's office. She sat behind her desk. On her left sat a man who appeared to be a doctor. It was Bill, the behavioral psychologist from human resources.

"Thanks for coming Bob, this shouldn't take too much time. Have you met Bill?"

"Yes I have. He's a company Psychologist. What's this about?"

Bill turned to Cynthia. "May I?" he said.

"Bob, Cynthia tells me your work has been erratic lately. Do you have difficulty meeting deadlines and performing tasks? Is that true?"

"I..., I don't think so. Some of my tasks are easy. Some require more time. Estimating labor hours in advance can be difficult when creativity is required."

"Yes, well you have missed some of your deadlines lately and you have been given a performance warning."

"We just want to make sure you understand the situation Bob. No one wants to see you underperform. You've always been quite capable in the past. In situations like this I have to consult with Bill, to make certain an employee isn't having problems. I asked him to perform a behavioral analysis."

"We performed a study using data recorded by your locator chip, we looked at the command history files from your robots, and of course your computer systems' history. The results seem to indicate you are having a problem. Do you feel you are having a problem? What solution would you suggest to resolve this problem?"

"I don't think I have a problem. I've never been happier. Today for example. The sunshine on the valley was so beautiful. I wish you could have seen it."

"Can you describe for us what your ideal job would be like?", said Cynthia.

"I don't understand the question. I've always been happy in this job."

"You have been spending a great deal of time outside Bob. Why are you going outside?", said Bill.

"It makes me feel good to get outside. I remember when I was a boy..., before everything became the way it is now."

"Are you unhappy with the way things are now? Do your feelings affect your work?"

"No. I honestly don't think my work has been affected."

"What do you do when you feel lonely?"

"I don't feel lonely. No more than anyone does nowadays. I do wish I could take another vacation. I think that could help."

"You have exhausted all your leave." said Cynthia, "And you still have deadlines to meet."

"How do you plan to resolve this situation, Bob?" Bill said.

"What exactly do you expect me to do?"

"We just want you to be proactive," said Cynthia.

After a long pause Cythia turned to Bill and said, "Do you have any more questions Bill?"

"Just one. Bob, can you tell me, how do you feel?"

The meeting dragged on for a while longer and it ended with Cynthia issuing a deadline that felt unfair. Bob felt terrible afterward, helpless. He knew he was good at what he did. The questions Bill had asked him made no sense. He lacked any frame of reference in which to answer them. He didn't understand how anyone could answer such questions truthfully and accurately. Did they want him to lie?

Should he take some anxiety medication? He knew that didn't help him in the long run. When he felt no anxiety he wanted more than ever to go outside. He wanted to experience the world again.

He went over to the window and looked out. The scene outside still looked serene and tranquil. It called to him. The thing he wanted most was to go outside and play like he did when he was a child.

"Arthur, I need for you to shut down. I want to check your power connections."

"What is the reason? I am functioning perfectly."

"Just a routine check. Better safe than sorry."

Arthur came forward to sit at the table, then he dutifully powered down. Bob looked around on his back, found the latch at the base of his neck, opened it and removed the power module.

Bob went to the back door and tried to open it. It would not open, not the outer door of the airlock. It could sense that he was not wearing his environment suit. He could open it, but it would set off the fire alarm. That would bring the fire department and they would make him go back inside.

He got the remote and his phone. As soon as he set off the alarm the door sprang open and he rushed outside. The air felt so warm, and a breeze, he had not felt a breeze in how long!

He shut off the alarm and the door slammed shut behind him. He had to hurriedly text the fire department and let them know it was a false alarm. He had dropped the remote

They believed him and issued the standard warnings. He promised to be a good boy and never do it again. Their authority restored, no one suspected that he had gone outside without his environment suit. It was illegal, but no one ever did it. At least, you never heard anything about it when they did. They didn't have to prevent anyone from doing it because everyone knew it was fatal.

Bob didn't care anymore. He wanted to feel his toes in the grass. He took off his shoes and slid his feet around in the tall grass, so good after all these years. He had to get to that creek!

He walked as fast as he could at first, then he trotted, when he got close enough to see it he ran the rest of the way. The sand! The gravel hurt his feet but he didn't care. He waded out into the water. It was cold! He forgot how cold it could be!

Bob had never been this happy in living memory. He wound up taking off his clothes and swimming in the creek. He was not afraid to die.

He didn't stop swimming and wading in the creek and trying to catch the minnows in his hands until the sun went down. Memories of his childhood and the way things were before overwhelmed him. He could have gone back to the house, but he refused.

He put on his clothes, found a patch of grass next to the bank and lay down. Stars were beginning to come out. How long had it been since he had seen them like this? He knew the rains and mists would come in after midnight and water the earth and him too but he didn't mind. He was going to sleep outside tonight! And not in an environment suit!

• • • • • • • • • • •

When Bob had not logged in to the corporation's computers for seventy-two hours the authorities were notified. The GPS chip implant in his wrist located him next to the creek. An observation satellite zoomed in on him with its telescopic camera. That gave them a positive identification.

When the emergency medical team found him, he lay peacefully on the grass, with a smile on his face.

Keeping the Door Locked

T he door was locked. Willis knew that the door was locked before he tried it. He couldn't help himself. He always tried doors to prove to himself they were locked. Every night before he went to bed he would go around, just as he was doing now, and check to make sure each door was locked. It was a habit he picked up long ago to make sure he never forgot anything or lost anything.

He kept his keys in his pants pocket at all times. Every time he walked toward or away from his car he would reach into his pocket to see if his keys were there. He even did it before getting into someone else's car.

Willis always locked his front door or back door or whatever door he left his house from as soon as he was outside. He had locked this door, his front door when he came home. He knew that, but he checked it anyway, just as he checked to see if it were locked after he entered earlier.

These habits started long ago, as far back as when he was a teenager, but certainly after he got out on his own. The first apartment he lived in his twenties got burglarized one day and that made matters worse. At some point, the Shadow Man began appearing in his dreams.

He thought back, he tried to remember when it started. It began gradually, the first dream he could remember for certain happened when he was in college. The dreams varied but the pattern remained the same. A dark figure like the shadow or silhouette of a man stood outside wherever he was sleeping. Sometimes it would stand outside his window. Sometimes he could sense it, could see the Shadow Man in the mind's eye of his dream standing outside his door, wanting to get in. Sometimes it did get in. Sometimes the Shadow Man got in the house, entered his room, and stood over him.

These dreams always terrified and angered Willis. He felt somehow that the Shadow Man was a burglar or home invader, or then at other times he felt that it was a supernatural figure. In any case, he felt he should fight it, he should defend himself, keep it outside or if it was already inside then he could kill the Shadow Man and it would be a justifiable homicide, self-defense.

But he could never move during these dreams, he couldn't even open his eyes. The most he could do sometimes was yell in his sleep, growl really. He could never really say anything, just make angry inarticulate snarls in an attempt to scare the intruder off.

Once in a while, he would wake up a girlfriend while having this dream or she would try to wake him up and he would start snarling at her. This always frightened his lovers when it happened and the incomplete explanations he would give didn't help. It was never the only cause of a breakup, but it contributed.

At one point he bought a twelve-gauge shotgun, the kind designed for home defense. He left it loaded with buckshot somewhere near, in a corner, or under the bed.

He remembered it during his dreams sometimes and thought in the dream state, "Can I reach it in time to defend myself?"

But he could never move so much as a finger toward it for fear of giving himself away. He knew the Shadow Man would see him go for his shotgun before he could get to it and overpower him. When the Shadow Man entered his room and he remembered his shotgun he would lie there thinking.

"I've got to get to my shotgun! But if I move he will know I am awake and will see me trying to get to it. It's too late to do anything!"

After he checked the front door and was certain it was locked, he walked back to his bedroom, shut the door tightly and locked it, undressed, and lay down. He had already gone through his nightly ritual of checking the doors and windows around the house, so he could relax now.

"I ought to get myself a dog.", he said aloud.

Presently he fell asleep. The dream began again after some time passed. This time it seemed more real than ever before. Willis felt that he was awake, that he had woken up in the middle of the night and lay in bed. He was certain of it.

The Shadow Man stood in his yard. He walked past the bedroom window casting his shadow across it in the moonlight and paused in front of the window for a while looking in. Willis could never see anything other than a black silhouette and that was all he could see now, but he was certain the Shadow Man could see him.

The Shadow Man moved away toward the front of the house. Willis could sense him outside the front door. Now he was inside the house. Now he was in the bedroom.

Willis lay as still as he could and pretended to be asleep. He was afraid to open his eyes. He could sense the Shadow Man standing over him. He was paralyzed with fright.

The Shadow Man brushed his shoulder to wake him. He couldn't open his eyes, he hoped he could still pretend to be asleep. It touched him again, gently on the shoulder. With great effort, he opened his eyes.

Willis looked up and saw himself. No longer a black silhouette but his own reflection stood over his bed looking down and smiling at him. The Shadow Man was Willis!

Then he woke up. Early morning twilight shone through the windows, but the room was empty and all the doors were locked.

The Man in the Wig

Wendell Bird stood outside his taxicab puckering his lips, lost in thought. He looked over the vacant lot in front of him, expecting the stray cats he fed each day to show up any minute. Lisa, the cab company's dispatcher, called to him over the CB radio mounted inside the cab. He could not hear her voice on the CB radio behind him, even though the door was open. He had lost some of his hearing over the years, and the rest of his hearing was selective. She was trying to get his attention so she could send him to pick up a customer who waited at home for a taxi to arrive, but she could not get a response from him. She was used to this kind of behavior from Wendell by now, but she had to keep trying as all the other taxi drivers were with customers. She also needed to make sure no foul play had occurred.

Wendell turned, opened the trunk and got out some loaves of bread and bags of cat food he had retrieved from a trash dumpster earlier that day. The stray cats plus a few domesticated ones emerged at the sight of this and began mewing at him, as if to hurry him up. He poured a pile of cat food on the ground and the cats eagerly gathered around. The bread he broke into pieces and spread about the vacant lot for the birds that would fly in later when it was safe.

Wendell wandered around, almost expression-less, except that on occasion, for no apparent rea-son, he puckered his lips as if blowing a kiss to someone in his mind's eye. He staggered a bit as he walked, his feet in worn shoes which didn't provide the support an elderly diabetic needed to prevent pain or damage to his feet. Perched on top of his head he wore a wig which needed cleaning and brushing out. The color of the wig, a dark brown, and the awkward placement of the wig on top of his head, made obvious the fact that, to any casual observer, it was a wig and not his real hair, and it did not make him look younger. Whether he wore it to cover a bald spot, to look young, or to keep his head warm, no one but Wendell knew.

While he went around feeding the cats and birds Lisa called to him every couple of minutes, knowing he would answer eventually. Lisa sat at her desk inside the cab stand with the telephones, radio, and paperwork in front of her, smoking a cigarette and eating a doughnut, answering the phone each time it rang and writing down the customer's information on the trip log sheets. She had worked at this job for twenty years and Wendell had already worked there for twenty years when she started. A creature of habit, he performed this cat feeding ritual every day.

Finally, he toddled back toward the open driver's side door and got close enough to hear her voice coming over the radio. He grabbed the microphone.

Octavia McGowan believed in the rules, and in following the rules. She taught English at a special education school for children with special needs. She had done so for twenty years. She attended the same Primitive Baptist Church she attended as a child and championed the doctrines of her Church. She lived by herself in a small apartment and used taxis to save money, believing cars to be an unnecessary expense.

Although she expected Cab Drivers to arrive on time, she never got completely ready to leave until they arrived. She preferred to putter about her apartment straightening, cleaning, this and that, up until the time the cab pulled up. She cleaned compulsively and had a fear of insects, particularly roaches. Her standard rule was that the driver should not honk when he pulled up. She told the dispatcher that it disturbed the neighbors, but the real reason was she thought it disrespectful, like a teenage boy honking for his date to come out instead of walking up to the door to meet the girl's Parents. She always requested that the cab arrive by a certain time, though she frequently changed her mind and called back, requesting that a cab would arrive sooner or later than her initial request. Complaints came easily to her.

As the time for her taxi approached she would check for its arrival by looking out the window. She refused to walk outside her door early, but she expected the driver to be there on time, never late, as tardiness was a violation of her principles. She taught her students that tardiness is a crime. She also expected that the driver would not run wait-time before she came out, to give her free time to get ready.

The pickup time she gave Lisa was close now, only ten minutes. She suspected the Driver would not arrive on time. Anger began to build within her at this Driver. She didn't know who it was yet, but she had a lecture prepared for him if he did not make it on time.

Cab Drivers were a suspicious lot to Mrs. Mc-Gowan. She did not know the full truth about them but she suspected much of it. A respectable church going Christian like her did not have personal experience with the habits and way of life of a Cab Driver, but she did know a great deal, and disapproved of what she did know about them.

If the Driver drove too fast, dressed in an unkempt fashion, smoked, did not follow instructions, or took her on a costly roundabout route, he was going to get an earful of reprimands. She decided she should call right now to find out where he was and remind the dispatcher to have him arrive at the appointed time. The dispatcher was expecting her call, because this happened every time Mrs. McGowan requested a cab. She had one thing in common with Wendell Bird; she was a creature of habit.

• • • ● ●● • ● • • • •

Wendell drove toward her apartment in no apparent hurry, in fact, driving too slow for the traffic conditions. His hearing and sight prevented him from driving in a safe and legal manner, but he had eluded detection and still retained a Taxi Driver's license. His Doctor, an old family friend, passed him on the paperwork he had to file every couple of years for his physical examination. The Cab Company owner, Lisa, and all the other Drivers knew about Wendell, but as long as he could get a Taxi License on his own, he would be allowed to drive. Anyone who could get a Taxi License could drive, as the owner wanted all his cabs on the road all the time.

Cars backed up behind him or angrily passed him on the right side as he crept down the left lane. Occasionally, he would step on the brakes if he thought someone followed him too closely.

He knew how to find her apartment. In spite of his age he could remember all the streets and the addresses of regular customers. By some accident he had never picked her up before. Probably due to the fact that once she found a driver she liked, she would make a special request for him each time. Lisa knew Mrs. McGowan would probably not like Wendell, but she had no choice but to send him since everyone else was busy, none of Mrs. McGowan's "special" Drivers were working, and the rest of the Drivers refused to take her anywhere. So today Mrs. McGowan would have to ride with Wendell Bird or call another Cab Company.

Wendell arrived on time, because Lisa sent him well ahead of time. He pulled in front of her apartment and loudly tapped the horn, contrary to her instructions and in violation of one of her primary rules. She jumped when she heard his horn, and called Lisa to complain. She was preparing to call anyway, because she always called a minute before time expecting her cab to arrive late.

"Tell him not to honk the horn!" she said. And again,

"Tell him to pull up and wait for me to come out, and don't honk the horn, and don't run no time!"

Wendell had already turned the meter on and was running wait-time on her, something he did with every customer. This habit frequently got him into trouble with customers, especially cost conscious customers like Mrs. McGowan. She looked out the slats on her sliding glass door and saw him sitting there with his meter lights on and began to get angrier. He is running time on me she thought to herself! She looked frantically around for her purse because she wanted to get outside as fast as she could, to make him shut the meter off.

Rushing for the door she heard him honk a second time. She opened the door but paused, feeling that she had forgotten something. A half second's thought and she knew what it was, her cell phone was lying on the kitchen counter where she left it after hanging up on Lisa. She left the door open, then bolted for her cell phone, grabbed it, and charged out on a mission. She knew that the Driver was running time on her and she was going to catch him at it and make him stop and give him a piece of her mind for doing it.

• • • ● ● • ● • ● • • •

Wendell sat in his cab in her driveway with his lips puckered, watching her door impatiently. He tapped his horn a second time just before she opened her door. After a few seconds an angry black woman bolted out the door then turned, closed it and began to dig furiously in her purse for her keys. She had yelled something at Wendell when she first walked out but he couldn't hear what she said. Quickly, she found them and bolted the door. Turning around she stared him down as she stomped toward the cab. It was now five minutes past her "time-call". Most Cab Drivers would allow that much time for a customer to come out and get in the cab before turning on the meter, but not Wendell. He would turn the meter on after arriving, time-call or no time-call.

"You better not be runnin' time on me!" she said after flouncing down in the back seat.

"It was a time-call ......," Wendell started to say but before he could finish.

"And *don't* honk your horn! I told Lisa to tell you not to honk!"

"Well I didn't know ......,"

"She didn't tell you that?"

"No, I didn't hear her say that ......,"

"Well don't do it!"

She sat fuming in the back seat; she had completely forgotten her reason for asking for a cab in the first place. Wendell, distracted by her tirade had forgotten to turn time off.

They sat in an uncomfortable silence for a few seconds when the dispatcher said over the radio.

"Did you get her Wendell?"

"Yeah, I got her."

"Where are you going?"

Wendell turned to Mrs. McGowan,

"Where do you want to go?"

"Take me to SVC!" she snapped, as if he should have known.

"We're going to SVC." Wendell announced.

He backed around slowly and started to turn the wrong way out of the parking lot.

"Where're you goin?"

"What?"

"SVC is that way!"

"Oh, Okay."

He paused for a while, because she was pointing out the direction to SVC behind his back where he could not see, and then he slowly pulled out in front of traffic into the center lane, in the right direction now, but at a snail's pace. The other cars obligingly missed hitting them but one tapped his horn as he passed.

"Didn't you see that car?" she said.

Wendell didn't respond but continued down the center lane until after a hundred feet or so he crept into the left lane with cars buzzing around him on the right side. When he was about to pass the Gasco Mrs. McGowan said,

"Stop here!"

"What? I thought you wanted to go to the SVC."

"Stop right here!"

"At the Gasco?"

"Right here!"

Wendell veered back into the center lane and crept forward until he could turn around and turn in. Mrs. McGowan would not admit it to anyone but she had one minor vice, she smoked cigarettes. She wanted to stop to buy a pack, and also get a newspaper for the coupons. She shopped almost exclusively with store coupons she got out of the newspaper.

He finally pulled up in front of the door of the Gasco after executing a u-turn and right turn in slow motion. Luckily, traffic had cleared and no one was coming. She looked at the meter before getting out so she could tell whether he had run wait-time on her when she got back.

"I'm only gonna be in there for a minute, you better not run no time."

"Okay." He lied.

As soon as she waddled out of the cab and into the convenience store, Wendell turned wait-time on. Technically, from a legal standpoint, it was the right thing to do, but some customers felt it was unfair, and Mrs. McGowan was one of them. But Wendell never considered what the customer thought, or how much more he might get tipped if he did not run wait-time for short stops. He ordinarily didn't receive tips from customers, and Mrs. McGowan didn't tip anyone, except at Christmas time she would give her regular Driver a whopping five dollars as a Christmas bonus.

He sat there watching the door so he could sneak time off when she came back out. Presently, she came back out, then remembering her newspaper; she turned to the newspaper rack. He snuck time off and then back on while she did this.

She returned to the cab clutching her newspaper and her bulky purse with her cigarettes safely hidden inside. After resuming her seat she looked at the meter. It had advanced a couple of dollars in her absence.

"You been runnin' time on me!"

"I've got to run wait-time ......,"

"I told you I'd be just a minute!"

"Well I didn't know how long you was gonna be in there, we've got to run wait-time on the customers when there're outside the cab."

She paused a moment and watched to see what his reaction was to her assault. She knew that it was the law that Cab Driver's not only could but must run wait-time, but that did not stop her from lobbying for whatever discount she could get. The Cab Driver had control over that portion of the meter and so could be bullied or persuaded not to run time. When she could see that it did not matter to Wendell what she said, she gave up.

Opening up her paper she pulled out the coupon section and began looking them over.

"You want to go to SVC now?"

"Hold on a minute, let me look at this."

If the bargains offered by another store appealed to her she would go there instead, or in addition to SVC. Wendell looked at the meter while she sat there reading the coupons, wasting his time, and biding her own time. He wanted to turn the meter back on wait-time but knew it would provoke her again.

"If you don't tell me where we're goin I'm gonna hafta run time."

"You just hold on a minute."

She found what she was looking for, coupons for SVC, Dollar Store, and Green's. After scrutinizing them a bit, she said,

"Take me to SVC."

Wendell put it in gear and headed cautiously out of the parking lot. After waiting a long time for traffic to clear he started to pull out.

Meanwhile, Mrs. McGowan, still steaming about the way he had started the meter as soon as he pulled up in her driveway, began to think of ways to make life difficult for Wendell. She noticed the wig he wore. You could not help but notice it sitting on his head as if some small animal had decided to lie down there.

The uncombed wig, with hair too dark to be Wendell's, together with his oddly matched clothing and shoes, created a comic appearance no one would intend. Wendell wore the wig in spite of questions and hints from friends who tried to help. Having found it in a dumpster, and needing some way to cover his bald spot, he wore it with pride, because he could not see well enough to tell by looking at himself in the mirror just how odd it looked. He had always preferred function over form in any case, since he tried to get by spending the smallest amount of money possible. Not because he didn't have money, he in fact had quite a lot, enough that he didn't need to drive a cab or dumpster dive. But Wendell, terrified of losing the money he did have, spent as little of it as possible.

The wig made him look crazy she thought, filthy and crazy. Only someone with bad habits and character flaws would go about dressed like that. How could the cab company and the city allow someone like Wendell to drive? Someone who dressed filthy and crazy and wore a wig like that and who ran time on people living on a budget before they could even pick up their purses and walk outside should have their license revoked. As many times as she had ridden with this company over the years, she felt entitled to better service. Lisa and the Company Owner were going to hear about this outrage.

In the meantime it was her duty to correct Wendell's behavior if she could. She could help him to reform, or she might at least make him feel bad about himself.

"What's that on yo head?" she said.

Wendell, concentrating to the best of his ability on the traffic could not clearly hear what she said but reacted to the tone of her voice by stomping on the brakes.

"What?" he said.

He stopped part way in and part of the way out of the parking lot, with his front wheels in the first lane of traffic. A car stopped abruptly, tires squealing to keep from hitting them, and then laid down on the horn after stopping.

"What you stopping in the middle of the street for, you gonna get us killed!"

The car paused for a while before pulling around, the driver made gestures at Wendell. Other cars trapped behind it came around until presently; traffic cleared enough for Wendell to pull out into the turn lane. He drove so slowly that Mrs. McGowan, her patience already short, felt she should complain again.

"Are you going to get us there some time today?"

Before Wendell could answer, the dispatcher's voice called to him over the radio.

"Wendell, did you just stop in the middle of the street in front of the Gasco?"

"I tried to pull out and this guy nearly ran into me!"

"Well somebody called me and said you stopped in the middle of the street."

During this exchange Mrs. McGowan continued to harass Wendell from the back seat, but he could neither hear her nor understand what she said. With too much going on for him to deal with he slowed down and stopped in the center lane and put it in park, but kept the engine running.

The dispatcher continued,

"You need to be careful out there and watch out for the other drivers."

"Well I did they just came flying out of nowhere!"

"Be careful!"

"Awright!"

He sat parked in the turning lane for a few moments of confusion, when Mrs. McGowan broke the silence.

"Are you going to take me to SVC or not?"

"Yeah, I'm goin' to."

Wendell eased out into the left lane and drove in the direction of SVC, this time without incident. Mrs. McGowan went back to busying herself with her sale papers. She did not notice how many cars passed them on the right side or how many cars got stuck behind them, their drivers burning with frustration.

When she looked up she saw a line of cars next to them and no one in front of them. She craned her neck to look behind her and saw cars stacked up behind them. The SVC loomed ahead on the right.

"Get over, You better turn over or you'll miss it!"

"I'm gettin' there as fast as I can, there's a lot of traffic out here."

"You the slowest driver I ever seen!"

Wendell put his blinker on and eased right. Miraculously, the cars in the right lane let him in, as much to avoid hitting him, as to avoid getting hit by him.

He made the right turn into the parking lot and pulled up in front of the door into an empty parking space. The whole maneuver took place like a roller coaster ride in slow motion. Mrs. McGowan remained quiet the entire time but only through great effort. Once they came to a complete stop she grabbed her purse and sale papers and said,

"I'll just be a minute, now don't you run that meter up while I'm gone."

She got out and waddled into the SVC taking her time as she went. Wendell immediately hit the "wait-time on" button on the meter as soon as her back was turned.

He sat there puckering his lips for a while, counting the bricks on the wall of the SVC. Some birds had nested up in the eaves and on the lettering of the drugstore; they fluttered about as he watched them. Wendell decided to get out and feed them.

He popped the trunk and got out and went around and began digging the leftover bread out of the trunk. After rummaging around a bit he produced a loaf and toddled back around to the sidewalk in front of the store to cast some bread crumbs around for the birds to feed on. The little birds, their hunger and their instinct to feed their young overcoming their fear, began to feed on the bread he cast about. A few drugstore customers passed by the funny man in the wig on their way into and out of the store, mistaking him for some homeless person in his mismatched clothes and oddly placed, uncombed wig.

His feet started to hurt, so he left the remainder of the bread on the sidewalk and went back to sit in the driver's seat of his taxi. He sat watching them, occasionally puckering his lips. It did not matter to him how long Mrs. McGowan took inside the store. Wendell felt a sense of contentment watching the birds feed. He did not need to drive a cab to survive, he had more than enough money to live on, money he had inherited. He enjoyed driving a cab and had done so for fifty years. Life for Wendell consisted of driving a cab and feeding the birds and stray animals. Everyone in the cab business knew about Wendell and his funny habits. Some loved him but most hated him or at least resented his presence, as they felt he took money away from cabbies that needed the money worse than he did.

Time passed and quite a flock of birds fed on the bread he left out. Mrs. McGowan fiddle faddled about inside the store while this went on, selecting her bargains carefully and pestering the store employees. Wendell continued to sit watching the birds with the windows of the cab rolled down and the trunk lid up, directly in the heat of the sun. He began to sweat and ripen in the sunlight. The interior of his cab usually needed cleaning because he would often keep the items he retrieved from local dumpsters on the front seat as well as in the trunk. Customers often complained about the smell, not only of the leftover food, but of Wendell as well. Sometimes, cockroaches had reportedly been seen in his cab. Cleaning and maintenance were not high priorities for Wendell as they would take time away from driving and making money. Afraid of missing customers and their money, Wendell hated to miss even a short trip. He would not take time to clean unless forced to, and mechanical problems with the cab went unreported.

Mrs. McGowan was not well liked either, even by her specials. She complained constantly, a combination of backseat driving and nit picking about whatever she could think of. She would sometimes ask questions to "get to know" a driver, then lecture him on his shortcomings. She never tipped.

The drivers she asked for as "specials" typically had the character of a teacher's pet. Some had been teacher's pets in school. These men would patiently grit their teeth and wait for the trip to end, or tell her jokes or gossip with her get her mind off her complaints. Some drivers refused to pick her up at all. One had notoriously put her out of his cab on the street after she backseat drove him beyond the limits of reason.

On weekdays she took cabs to and from school, often with a stop at a drug store or dollar store along the way. On weekends she went on her long shopping trips. On Sunday she went to Church. She both blessed and cursed those she selected as her drivers, as she regularly took long cab rides for big money, but she did not tip and put everyone through hell.

When she came back outside rolling her cart she saw Wendell sitting in the cab with the windows down and the trunk lid up. He made no effort to get out. A small flock of birds gathered on the sidewalk in front of the taxi. A few droppings appeared on the hood of the cab and the sidewalk. She wheeled her cart toward the open trunk lid to unload her purchase, miffed that Wendell did not move to help.

When she saw the contents of the trunk she blew her top. Stashed inside were bags of cat food, stale loaves of bread and packages of doughnuts, various other unidentified packages that appeared to be food. She stomped around to where Wendell sat with his lips puckered.

"What is all that stuff in your trunk!"

"Oh, that's just a few things I picked up you know."

"Get it out of there! I've got to put my things in and I'm not mixin' it in with yo' trash!"

Wendell gathered himself and went around and began moving things from the trunk to the passenger side of the front seat. As he did, roaches scurried off some of the bags and hid themselves in the cab or deeper inside the bags. Mrs. McGowan did not see the roaches as she had her attention fixed on Wendell as she watched disapprovingly with her hands gripping her cart.

"You not puttin' that in the cab are you?"

"Well, I've got to put it somewhere; I just can't throw it away."

"It looks like somebody already throwed it away and you found it in the trash!"

She did not realize how right she was. Wendell had in fact dug all those things out of dumpsters, either that morning or earlier in the week. He finished piling things up on the passenger seat, on the floor, and on the dashboard and turned to watch her.

She went over and inspected the trunk. The roaches had hidden themselves; all that remained were some bread crumbs and a slight smell. She quickly unloaded her cart and slammed the trunk lid, then rolled her cart noisily back to the store entrance. It occurred to her that she might want to cut her trip short, but she still wanted to get something at the Dollar Store that she couldn't get anywhere else, at least, not without a coupon.

"Take me to the Dollar Store."

She said after resuming her place in the back seat. Once again, Wendell slowly backed out and crept across the parking lot. Luckily, he did not have to make a left turn this time. He turned right after all the cars had passed, and then ran the red light in slow motion. Cars rushing out into the intersection suddenly stopped and honked angrily but left enough room for him to get through.

"Can't you see where you are goin'!"

A feeling of indignation built inside Mrs. McGowan. In the past, she had had trouble with Cab Drivers, but mainly because of her high standards and her quickness to correct behavior. This Driver was unlike any she had seen before. Everything about Wendell violated acceptable standards. He should not be allowed to drive, she concluded. She was going to complain to the Cab Company and the City and have him removed.

A police car drove past in the opposite direction and she started to wave at the officer to get his attention, but thought better about it. She would wait until after the trip was over or maybe if she saw someone at the store. She definitely had made up her mind to do something, as soon as she could.

She started digging in her purse to find her cell phone and call Lisa. She began rummaging around in all the compartments but could not find it. She tried sorting through and under everything else in her purse as quickly as she could but no cell phone. She looked on the seat and the floor of the taxi in case she dropped it there, but no luck. She wanted to dump the contents out to spread everything out but was afraid to do that; it would have to wait until she could get to the next store. She turned her attention back to Wendell.

The events that took place outside SVC had so distracted her that she forgot to notice that Wendell had run time on her, or check to see how much money the meter currently had on it. Wendell's wig had become more disheveled; it appeared to be on backwards.

"You got that wig on backwards", she said.

"What?"

"You got that wig on backwards, and you need to brush it out, Why you wearin' that thing anyway?"

Her habit was to dominate any conversation, so she tended to ask questions and make statements without waiting for a reply. Absurdly, she did expect answers, but impatience prevented her from listening to them. She expected to hear excuses in any case. This method of communication made it impossible to talk about anything other than her opinions, but she did not care. The excuses of students and cab drivers did not interest her. She simply expected them to follow her rules.

Wendell merely puckered up his lips and looked annoyed as he squinted at the traffic in front of him. He drove like a man trying to find his way through a Gulf Coast thunderstorm, as if visibility were so low that all you could see was the taillights of the car in front of you, but the sun shown brightly. He hunched forward as if it required all his concentration to travel at thirty miles per hour. If Mrs. McGowan had not felt so much anger, she would have felt fear. Most customers reported feeling fear after riding with Wendell.

They arrived at the Dollar Store in much the same manner as they arrived at SVC earlier. Cars tailgated and honked their horns as Wendell slowly turned in and parked. Pedestrians walked out in front of him not realizing that he could not see them until they were directly in front of him.

"You better not run time like you did last time."

She said as a parting shot before disappearing into the Dollar Store. He turned time on as soon as her back was turned. Wendell would argue or fight with the customers when he felt he needed to, but he had learned to pick his battles.

The Dollar Store's trash dumpster sat on the left side of the store, easily visible from where he sat waiting for her to finish shopping. It sat there over-flowing with garbage. Who knew what treasures lay inside it? It got Wendell's attention as soon as he turned around and noticed it. He stared at it a long time, and then he grabbed the CB radio microphone.

"Steppin' out of the cab"

"Ten four Wendell"

Wendell got out and shuffled over and looked inside. He rearranged things carefully so as not to move something out of reach. He wound up pulling some things out and laying them on the ground. Soon, he uncovered a gold mine of baked goods that had gone past their freshness dates. He found packages of miniature doughnuts mostly, plus hot dog and hamburger buns. Taking them out, he set them on the ground in a different spot than the garbage he had to remove to get to them.

A pile of discarded snack cakes remained at the back of the dumpster, out of reach. Wendell stood there a long time, wondering what to do. He wanted to get to them so badly but he no longer possessed the agility to climb in and get them out. He kept looking at the garbage stuffed in between to see if there was not some way to move it so he could reach the snack cake boxes.

This obsession with the snack cakes went on long enough that Mrs. McGowan finished her shopping and came back outside the store. She wheeled no cart this time, but carried a couple of plastic shopping bags. Getting close to the cab, she could see no one inside it. She turned around but did not see Wendell right away. She was not going to pay for time while a driver was not in the cab she thought to herself.

"I'm gonna turn that meter off, this is ridiculous!"

She said out loud as if anyone who could hear her should be informed of this outrage. Trying the door though, she found it locked. Wendell had long ago acquired the habit of locking up the cab behind him to prevent customers from doing what she planned to do.

Over by the dumpster, Wendell got that feeling of having someone stare at you from behind. He turned to see Mrs. McGowan standing beside the cab. That made him grab up his doughnuts as fast as he could and start toward the cab. Before he left the dumpster she spotted him and prepared to do battle.

When he got close enough she said, "You not puttin' those things in this cab!"

"What?"

"I saw what you did! You got that stale trash out of that dumpster! You not puttin' that garbage in this cab while I'm ridin' in it!"

Wendell stood there stunned, trying to think fast. He could not bear to leave such bounty behind, but he knew she meant what she said. He had to think of a way to talk her into letting him take it with them.

"They're not stale; they just threw them out today because of the freshness date you know. You can have some if you want."

"I'm not gonna eat somethin' that came out of a dumpster! You crazy! Put those things back in that dumpster and open up this cab and turn the meter off!"

Wendell hesitated, he really did not want to lose the doughnuts, but he knew she meant business. He looked around at the dumpster hoping for a place to stash them until he could come back to retrieve them. Before he could do anything she said,

"You put those nasty things down and open up this cab and stop runnin' time on me! I'm not payin' you to mess around in that dumpster while I wait!"

"Okay! Okay! Keep your shirt on I'm comin'!"

At a loss, he set them on the sidewalk and started toward the cab.

"You can't leave them there! That's litterin'!"

"Well, do you want me to turn time off or not?"

He had her there, so she said, "Unlock this cab, turn time off, and then throw that trash away!"

He unlocked the cab and reached in and hit the time off button. She got in and sat fuming while he went back and gathered up the doughnuts and tod-dled back toward the dumpster area looking about for a place to stash them as he went.

He saw an empty cart around the side of the dumpster. Wendell put the doughnuts there, and then wheeled it around behind the dumpster where no one could see it. He toddled back to the cab. When he got back in she confronted him again.

"Did you get all that stuff out of a dumpster?"

She was talking about his stash of stuff in the front seat. He would not leave it behind as well, so he thought fast.

"No, they give them to me; people give me what they are going to throw out anyway."

"You better not be lyin' to me, I'm going to tell the owner of this cab company what you did."

That bit of news did not worry Wendell at all, since the owner and everyone else knew about his peculiar habits. He cranked the cab up.

"You want to go back home now?"

"No, I want you to take me to Green's."

That news disappointed him as he had become tired of her by now and wanted to get back to his stash as soon as possible, but he had nothing left to do but finish his trip and collect his money. He put it in reverse and started to back out, but a driver honking their horn as he started back made him stop suddenly.

"Can't you see what you're doing?"

"Yeah, I can see, but these people speed through here all the time."

He finished backing out slowly and pulled around to turn out into the street. Mrs. McGowan had rattled him so badly that he had forgotten which direction to turn to get to Green's. Wendell turned the wrong way and headed into traffic. Mrs. McGowan knew that he had turned the wrong way but she waited before pouncing.

"You are goin' the wrong way!"

"What? You said you wanted to go to Green's."

"Green's is that way!"

"Huh! What are you talkin' about?"

"Turn this cab around! You goin' the wrong way!"

Wendell then pulled off a minor miracle. Starting from the right lane he executed a u-turn into the right lane of traffic going in the opposite direction. The whole thing happened in slow motion with cars braking and honking and Mrs. McGowan screaming incoherently from the back seat. Oblivious to anything she said now, he only wanted to get the trip over. She could not deter him from finishing the trip the way he thought best. He had fifty years of experience as a cab driver and she had rattled him, but nothing could change his way of doing things. He resumed driving as he had before, this time in the correct direction.

Mrs. McGowan felt a change taking place within herself. Before, she had felt little else but anger and contempt for this crazy old man in the wig. Now, she felt fear for her life.

"Let me out of this cab!"

Wendell appeared not to hear her as he crouched forward over the steering wheel, intent on finishing the trip. So she insisted.

"Pull this cab over and let me out!"

In spite of his advanced age Wendell knew exactly what to say and do in these situations.

"I'll let you out at the Green's, and you have to pay me whatever's on the meter when we get there."

"Let me out now! And tell them to send me another cab!"

"I can't stop here in the middle of the street!"

Mrs. McGowan had nearly reached the point of hysteria and was going to continue to insist he pull over, when she saw the Green's across the intersection in front of them. Hope entered her heart when she saw they were nearly there. She decided to let him put her out at Green's and have the company send another driver when it was time to take her home. If only she could make it there in one piece with this crazy, blind, and deaf old man behind the wheel.

She closed her eyes and prayed silently. She could not see that as they approached the intersection the light was about to change. Mrs. McGowan felt something crawling on her. Opening her eyes she saw a large cockroach, one of the roaches that had entered the cab on Wendell's food, on her skirt. It looked up at her waving its antennae. She had been afraid of insects ever since childhood. Even in her present state of mind she knew exactly where this roach was from and that there were others in the cab with her. A piercing scream rose from deep within her; a scream so loud that it startled Wendell even though he had difficulty hearing. He reflexively turned, and took his eyes off the road, so he did not see the light change from yellow to bright red, or see the semi-tractor trailer rig that bore down on the intersection with the logo of the Dollar Store they had just visited painted on its side.

The truck driver continued toward the intersection at a speed of fifty-five miles per hour as the light turned green ahead of him. The truck driver did not have time to take his foot off the accelerator to apply the brakes when the cab appeared in front of him. The image of a cab driven by an old man in a wig with a woman trying desperately to exit the back seat of a moving vehicle was imprinted on the truck driver's memory in the final fraction of a second before impact.

The momentum of the collision pushed the cab completely through the intersection and sent it spinning into a three hundred sixty degree turn. The semi-truck jackknifed. Mrs. McGowan was thrown clear, receiving only road rash and a concussion. The truck driver was not charged and resumed his duties after hospitalization for his injuries and a leave of absence while the Department of Transportation conducted an investigation. The cockroach survived the accident and went on to lay hundreds of eggs in a local dumpster.

· · ● ● ● · ● ● · · ·

Wendell Bird stood looking out over the vacant lot where he fed stray cats every day, puckering his lips as he surveyed the scene. Behind him sat his old car with its trunk lid missing, its passenger side window replaced by a piece of plastic, filled with an odd assortment of junk.

Wendell turned to the trunk with its missing lid and got out some loaves of bread and bags of cat food he had retrieved from a trash dumpster earlier that day. The stray cats plus a few domesticated ones emerged at the sight of this and began mewing at him, to hurry him up. He poured a pile of cat food on the ground and the cats eagerly gathered around. The bread he broke into pieces and spread about the vacant lot for the birds that would fly in later when it was safe.

Lisa's voice did not call to him as he did not have a CB radio. The mewing and purring of cats were the only sounds he could hear. Wendell felt serene, but something was missing now. He puckered his lips.

He would drive by the Cab Stand afterward and ask for his old job back, as he did every day, and Lisa would try to explain to him that he wasn't allowed to drive anymore.

The Day All the Libraries Closed

For Willis Weatherington, the day was like any other. He slept until about eight o'clock. He didn't feel well when he got up, the damn hotel mattress was too soft or something. On a typical day, he woke up with soreness in his muscles to remind him that he lived in a cheap hotel and didn't make enough money to move yet.

The place was noisy too. You could hear the neighbors upstairs stomping around and scraping chairs across the floor every time they moved. You could hear the next-door neighbors bumping against the walls and they had a colicky baby that cried day and night.

Willis was one of those highly sensitive people who couldn't bear such noises. He wanted more than anything else to be a science fiction writer and he felt the world was conspiring against him.

He struggled, believing that a writer, himself, in any case, needed quiet and solitude to practice his art undisturbed. He never watched television. Friends and family had been left behind. Willis simply stopped contacting them or visited the places where he used to find company. He didn't want to discuss what he was doing with anyone until he had been published.

There would, of course, be some who would criticize him anyway, but he wouldn't care. He would have the external validation he needed. He could show them the magazine the story was printed in, show them the story itself, read it to them if necessary or email them a samizdat copy.

On a typical morning, he would wake a little early from the noise upstairs or the noise next door, feel a little despair and fall back asleep to nightmares about frustration and persecution. Willis knew intellectually that the other hotel guests were utterly thoughtless, but he couldn't help feeling that they knew somehow what they were doing and the effect it had on him. They were doing it on purpose, out of envy or something.

The universe simply didn't want him to write.

The solution to this problem was the local library. It opened at nine in the morning and closed at nine at night and contained rooms and corners he could hide in. It was noisy too of course. Not like the libraries of his childhood when elderly ladies stood guard and shushed anyone who spoke too loudly.

The library workers were as often as not the culprits. They carried on loud animated conversations with library patrons. One time, a custodial worker actually walked through the library whistling a song. Willis stared a hole through him but the custodian showed no recognition of his behavior.

There were of course solutions: earplugs, noise-canceling headphones. These would have worked at home as well but Willis felt depressed when he stayed home to write. His room made him feel cooped up.

He got up and performed his stretches and breathing exercises. He regarded himself in the mirror. Gray thinning hair, a beer belly, but still a youthful-looking face. He would go to the library and work on his story all day today. Not just a page or two for a few hours.

"I will finish a story and send it off!" he told his reflection.

He dressed quickly and went downstairs through the lobby. No one was in the lobby or the hallway thank god. The other guests, total strangers, always wanted to engage in idle chit chat, or to ask him for money, or to proposition him sexually. He could never tell what they wanted beforehand, whether innocent or vile, so he preferred not speaking at all. What had happened to the culture he wondered? People didn't act this way when he was a child, they were polite.

The hotel desk clerk was not behind the counter. It upset him to speak to her. He wanted to be nice to her, he needed her cooperation at times but she inevitably made sexual innuendos. He didn't like, had never liked, for women to be forward, and the fact that she knew where he lived and could enter his room at any time created the possibility of an unwanted intrusion.

What if they broke up acrimoniously? What if she turned out to be crazy? It seemed likely not to end well. She was not there so he rushed on through the lobby; out into an almost empty parking lot.

When Willis got to the library it was closed. This seemed odd considering it was an ordinary Monday morning. But there were no cars in the parking lot except for a few that might belong to maintenance personnel, or perhaps had been abandoned. He decided to try the door.

There was a notice that read:

"THE PUBLIC LIBRARY, ALONG WITH THE CITY GOVERNMENT, HAS BEEN CLOSELY MONITORING THE RECOMMENDATIONS BY LOCAL, STATE, AND NATIONAL OFFICIALS REGARDING THE **THREAT**. IN AN ABUNDANCE OF CAUTION AND FOR THE SAFETY OF OUR CITIZENS AS WELL AS OUR STAFF, THE PUBLIC LIBRARY WILL BE CLOSED UNTIL FURTHER NOTICE."

Willis cursed his luck. He felt surprised and confused at this turn of events. Where could he go to write? He was the only one there. No one else was there to get in. If some staff were inside they were hiding.

"What **THREAT**?", he wondered aloud.

The town he lived in sometimes experienced tornado outbreaks and sometimes ice storms, but that day's weather gave no hint of an approaching storm of any kind. When these storms were predicted people panicked and did the same inexplicable things each time. They stripped the shelves of grocery stores of bread and milk as if preparing for a long blackout.

The only thing to do was try the library in the next town over, then if it was closed too he could try a coffee shop. He didn't like the thought of that, it would mean more noise and importunities. He would have to use his earplugs but he would still get bothered by the customers and employees.

When Willis arrived at the next little suburban town's library he found the same circumstance as before. A parking lot empty save for a few vehicles that may have belonged to the staff. No one there trying to get in, and a sign on the front door which read:

"DUE TO THE **THREAT**, THE LIBRARY WILL BE CLOSED INDEFINITELY."

What on earth could this be about? What was this **THREAT** that had shut down two libraries? It was tempting to turn on a television to find out or check social media, or just ask someone on the street. He didn't like to do anything like that first thing in the morning though. It would poison his unconscious mind, disturb the writing process. He had eliminated all morning distractions in an effort to create a morning routine that would make him a successful writer.

For that matter, where are all the people? The streets were nearly empty and there was no one there. He looked through the glass doors and saw no one. He started pounding on them with his hand. The lights inside were just as you would leave them for a routine closure. He went around to the side windows and looked in. If the staff were inside they were hiding from him.

He gave up.

"I'll try the coffee shop," he said. He was beginning to talk to himself.

•　•　●　●　●　•　●　●　●　•　•

The same conditions were present at the coffee shop. This time a completely empty parking lot and a sign that read:

"CLOSED UNTIL FURTHER NOTICE DUE TO THE **THREAT**."

Willis began to feel a lump in his throat. Something weird was going on. Whatever this **THREAT** was it was real or was believed to be real by the majority of the public and the local authorities and it was something out of the ordinary, not the weather.

Had there been some kind of attack or was one imminent? It gave him an idea. A post-apocalyptic novel! Considering how the public was reacting to the **THREAT** a post-apocalyptic novel might sell quite well! His trip was not entirely wasted.

Willis went back to the hotel. He entered through the side door to avoid the overly talkative desk clerk. The parking lot had emptied out considerably. Are people leaving because of the **THREAT**? This could turn out to work to my advantage Willis thought.

When Willis got to his room he opened the door carefully, stood inside and listened. It was quiet! There was no sound of stomping feet or furniture being moved upstairs. There was no bumping against the wall or sounds of a television playing next door. It felt peaceful.

Willis began to hope. Can this be true at last? Will I be able to write here in this room undisturbed? Dare I to hope?

He went immediately to his computer. He began to work. He worked for at least ninety minutes without any kind of noise and interruption. He got up and paced the floor a little and listened, taking it all in.

It was quiet at last! He began to relax, to feel a sense of accomplishment. He would not have to go anywhere. He could finish his novel right here in his room without leaving if this happy state of affairs lasted. Willis sat down on his bed and dreamed of how he would stay in his room and write undisturbed as the **THREAT** continued. He lay back and drifted into a reverie and fell asleep.

A loud knock on the door startled him awake.

"Front desk! Mr. Weatherington are you in there?"

It was the too friendly desk clerk. Willis got up and staggered to the door. The young woman stood there and a police officer was with her.

"We need for you to vacate your room Mr. Weatherington.", she said.

"What? Why? What's going on?"

"Because of the **THREAT** we are going to have to shut the hotel down and relocate all the guests to secure areas.", the policeman said.

"What is this **THREAT**? Has there been some kind of attack? Are you expecting some kind of attack?"

"Haven't you heard? You need to get out more!", she said and laughed. "You should stop to talk to me more often."

"Look I've got work to do here I can't leave!"

"Just pack a change of clothes and some toiletries. You can leave the rest of your belongings here, they will be safe until you return.", the policeman said.

"When I return! When will I return?"

"We don't know yet," she said. "Look Willis everyone's got to do it or the **THREAT** could get much worse."

"I need to take my laptop with me."

"I'm afraid that's not possible Mr. Weatherington. Space will be limited so you can only bring the things I mentioned.", the officer said.

"The same rules apply to everyone.", she said.

"But I need to write! I've got to finish my novel!"

"I'm afraid you've got to come with us now!", the officer said and came into the room. The desk clerk came in with him. Willis walked back over and slumped down on the bed, hanging his head.

"We'll help you pack, don't worry.", she said.

When they were through packing they all went downstairs and outside to where the police car waited for Willis and the officer.

Willis turned to them and asked, "Will I at least have a room of my own?"

"Yes, everyone will be confined to a room of their own for the duration of the **THREAT** Mr. Weatherington. But it's not very big.", she said.

"Is it quiet there? I need a place that's quiet," said Willis.

"I'm sure it's quiet most of the time."

"Good," said Willis.

Maybe I can get them to let me have a notebook and a pen he thought to himself. He knew that he had to find a way to write no matter what, but he knew somehow that he wouldn't be able to.

About Author

Born in Mobile, Alabama, V. H. Mizzell spent the entirety of his childhood there, except for the sixth grade in Summit, New Jersey.

He holds a BS in Physics from Auburn University and almost but not quite an MS in Mathematics from UAH.

He has spent thirty years in the Defense/Aerospace industry, most notably working as a Fortran programmer on the Burst and Transient Source Experiment (BATSE) and as a Systems Engineer for the Boeing Company, Lockheed Martin, and Northrup Grumman.

He developed a love of Science Fiction when he found Heinlein's juvenile series in the Mobile Public Library Bookmobile. That was also the year that Star Trek premiered and his big sister bought a telescope.

Also By V. H. Mizzell

To See Beyond Tomorrow (The History of the Psychics, Book One)